CW00738856

Little Hoglet's Christmas

Richard Middleton

First Edition

ISBN-13: 978-1522942573
ISBN-10: 1522942572

For Finn

Little Hoglet is fast asleep in his lovely warm bed. Suddenly...

"HO!

HO! HO!"

...he is woken by the most curious sound. What is it?

Little Hoglet leaps out of bed to investigate.

He can't
believe it!

The whole world has turned white.

But Little Hoglet
is too excited to
go back to bed.

What a wonderful sight! Two stoats in their winter coats dancing all night.

"No! No! No! Tonight it will snow, snow, snow! Go back to bed, Little Hoglet!"

But Little Hoglet is
too excited to listen.

Soon it does begin
to snow, snow, snow.

Little Hoglet feels cold, cold, cold.

Soon he will freeze, freeze, freeze!

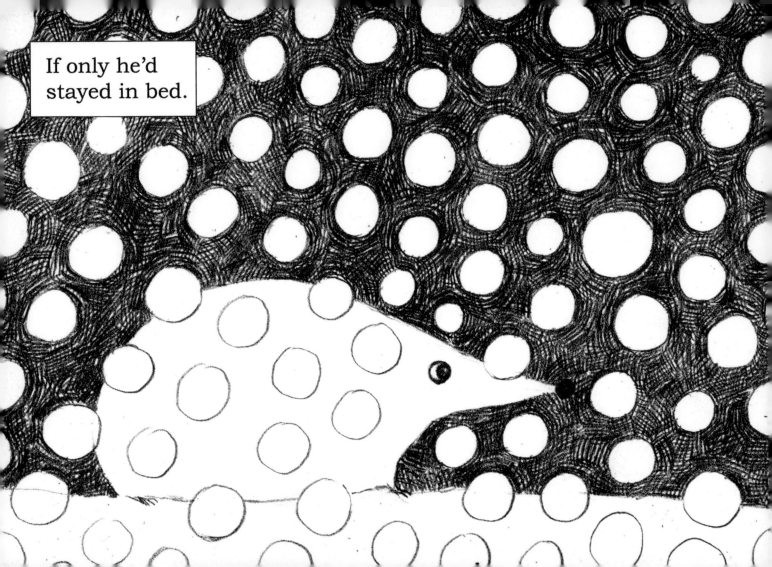

If only he'd stayed in bed.

What's this?

The beautiful tree makes
Little Hoglet feel very happy.

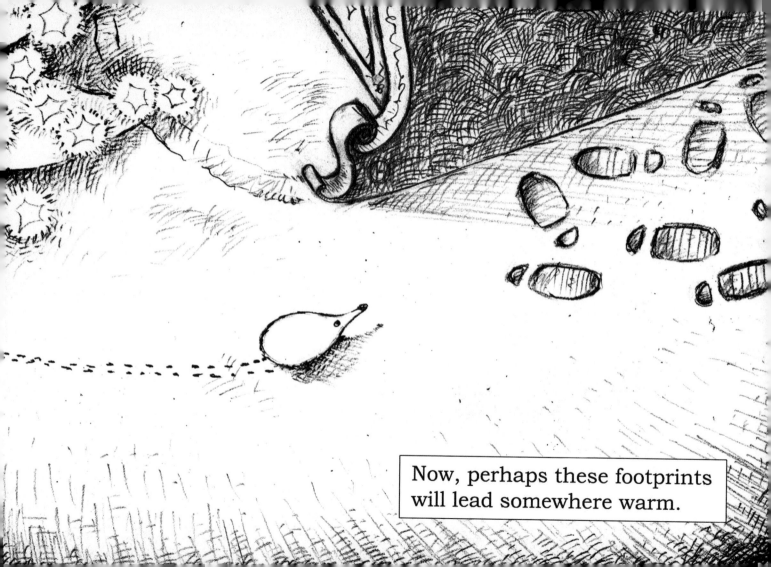

Now, perhaps these footprints will lead somewhere warm.

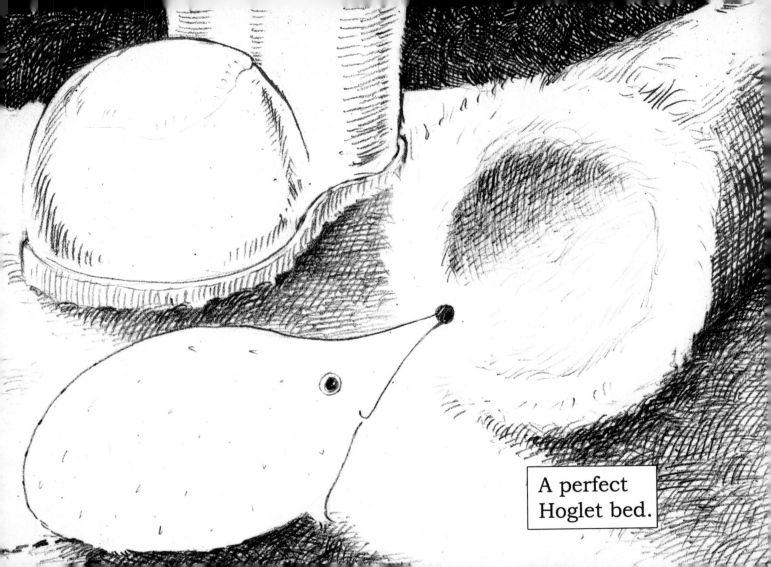

A perfect
Hoglet bed.

"Hello, Mr Ho! Ho! Ho!"

"I'm warm and cosy now. Goodnight!"

"Goodnight,
Little Hoglet."

"Happy Christmas!"

...Little Hoglet dreams very Happy Christmas dreams!

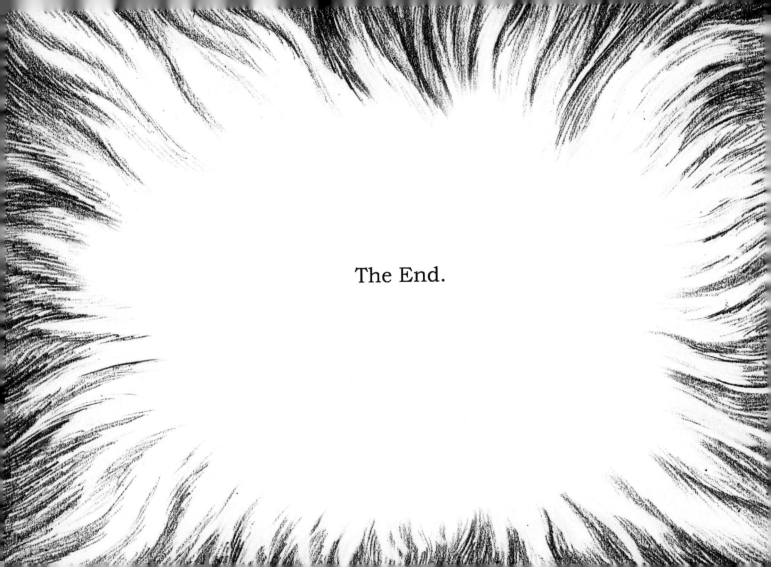

The End.

Printed in Great Britain
by Amazon